EARTH
SONGS

EARTH SONGS

Myra Cohn Livingston, Poet

Leonard Everett Fisher, Painter

Holiday House/New York

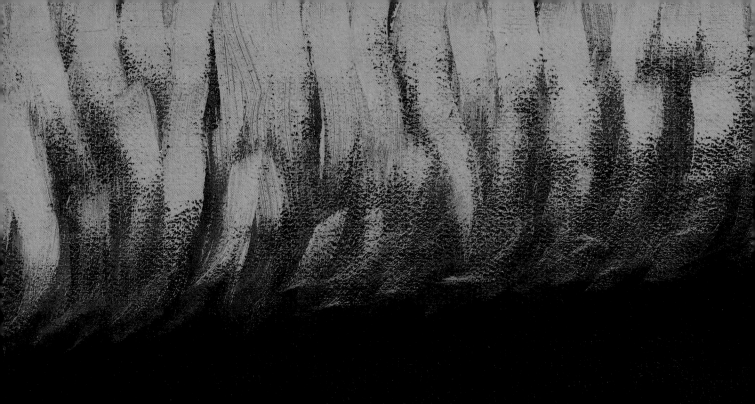

For Anna and Pieter-Jan
January 18, 1986
M. C. L.

Text copyright © 1986 by Myra Cohn Livingston
Illustrations copyright © 1986 by Leonard Everett Fisher
All rights reserved
Printed in the United States of America
First Edition

Library of Congress Cataloging-in-Publication Data

Livingston, Myra Cohn.
Earth songs.

SUMMARY: A poetic tribute to that little O, the earth,
its continents, clay, hills, forests, and seas.
1. Earth—Juvenile poetry.   2. Children's poetry,
American. [1. Earth—Poetry.   2. American poetry]
I. Fisher, Leonard Everett, ill.   II. Title.
PS3562.I945E3   1986   811'.54   86-341
ISBN 0-823

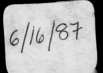

"The little O, the earth."

WILLIAM SHAKESPEARE,
Antony and Cleopatra
Act V, Scene ii

Little O, small earth, spinning in space,
face covered with dizzy clouds, racing,
chasing sunlight through the Milky Way,
say your secrets, small earth, little O,
know where you lead, I follow. I go.

Patched together
With land and sea,
I am earth,
Great earth.
Come with me!

Huge continents lie on me, dry land,
sand grained from crumbled rock, now drifted,
sifted to powder. Silt, sand, red clay
weigh down my crust in layers of loam.
Roam everywhere—I am earth, your home.

Uplands clamber over me, climb high
skyward. Hummocks, hillocks, small knolls
roll in circles, slope and tumble down.
Round hills rise to bluffs. My highlands change—
Range over me! Look! My shapes grow strange.

Mountains rise above me, their slopes white,
bright with fresh snow, tall peaks glistering.
Blistering brown domes bend over, hunched,
bunched together. Some, chained in deep folds,
molded in waves, sleep, wrinkled and old.

Hot volcanoes breathe in me, my back
blackened with cinders, scars of old fires,
pyres of ash. My red mouth and throat burn,
churn with hot, liquid lava. Below
flow molten rivers. Turn away! Go!

Forests live on me. Tall evergreens
lean against my mountains. Stands of beech
reach to the sky. Huge timber and bark
darken my leaf-strewn floors. Oak, teak, and pine,
vine-twisted rain forests—all are mine.

Waters bathe me, splash over my shores.
Pouring down from springs, ribboned streams
gleam with rills, hurry downwards, dashing,
plashing. Rivers rise. Blue swells leap high.
Dry up my waters and I will die.

Tundra covers me; swamps sodden, dank,
banked with moss, a soft, spongy morass.
Grassy bogs blanket my soaked crust here.
Sere, barren plains slush through marshes found
mounded with sedge on wet, withered ground.

Lowlands slide down me. Dip and hollow
follow the path to dell and ravine,
careen to broad valley, rocky gorge,
forge giant fissures. My canyons deep
sleep in stone walls, black, silent and steep.

Deserts sleep on me, restless, shifting,
drifting mounds of sand whipped by dry wind.
Skinned and barren, these dun, arid dunes
strewn with scorched tumbleweed, slumber, cursed,
submersed in mirage and endless thirst.

Under my granite crust, in dark halls,
walls store minerals, oil, layered shale,
pale gems, crystals, beds of coal. In caves
graves of fossiled rock and iron ore—
more than can be told. Go down! Explore!

Changed by ice and water, I am worn,
torn apart by glaciers. Rivers drink,
sink my stones, eat sand, soil, bathe in mud.
Flood steals my rocks. Wind erodes me. Then
when ocean floors fill, I rise again.

Big O, great planet, spinning in space,
face covered with dizzy clouds, racing,
chasing sunlight through the Milky Way,
say your secrets again, giant O.
Know where you lead, I follow. I go.

Patched together
With land and sea,
I am earth,
Little O.
Come with me!